Table of Contents

1.Title: THE LIFE OF BLACK AMERICAN

2.Copyright

3.Introduction:

One of the major ethnic groupings in the United States are the African Americans. Although most African Americans are of African descent, many also have non-African forebears. They are descended from slaves who were transported forcibly from their native Africa to do harsh work.

For a very long time, their rights were denied a fair portion of the economy. Basic and enduring contributions made by African Americans to American history and culture. Some Africans themselves sold captives to European merchants as enslaved persons and slavery became more and more profitable.

For the dreaded middle journey across the Atlantic Ocean, mainly to the West Indies, the abducted Africans were often chained to the shore and packed into the holds of slave ships.

At least one-sixth of those who died while crossing the border did so as a result of shock, illness, or suicide.

4.Storyline:

Early on in their discovery of America, Africans helped the Spanish and the Portuguese. In the 26th century, several black explorers settled in the Mississippi valley. As a result of evolutionary pressures favoring the presence of a dark pigment called melanin in the skin of populations in equatorial climates from the rest of the population, 20 Africans were easily distinguishable by their skin color in 1619, marking them as a highly visible target for enslavement.

5. Photo Activities:

A SLAVE-HUNT.

INSPECTION AND SALE OF A NEGRO.

TIPO TIB'S FRESH CAPTIVES BEING SENT INTO BONDAGE—WITNESSED BY STANLEY.

6. About us:

Because of the way their complexion has been seen in comparison to others, Black Africans have been reduced to slavery. Esteban, who explored the southwest in 1530, is the most renowned black American explorer.

www.ingramcontent.com/pod-product-compliance
Lightning Source LLC
LaVergne TN
LVHW020545160826
845677LV00015B/4221

* 9 7 9 8 8 4 6 1 3 7 0 8 0 *